With

to
Richard P. Gross

Reinforced binding of hardcover edition suitable for library use.

Copyright © 1987 by Ruth Heller. All rights reserved.
Published by Grosset & Dunlap, Inc., a member of The Putnam
& Grosset Group, New York. Published simultaneously in Canada.
Sandcastle Books and the Sandcastle logo are trademarks belonging to
The Putnam & Grosset Group. First Sandcastle Books edition, 1992.
Printed in Singapore. Library of Congress Catalog Card Number: 87-80254
ISBN (hardcover) 0-448-19211-X F G H I J
ISBN (Sandcastle) 0-448-40451-6 C D E F G H I J

A Cache of Jewels

and Other Collective Nouns

Written and illustrated by
RUTH HELLER

GROSSET & DUNLAP, NEW YORK

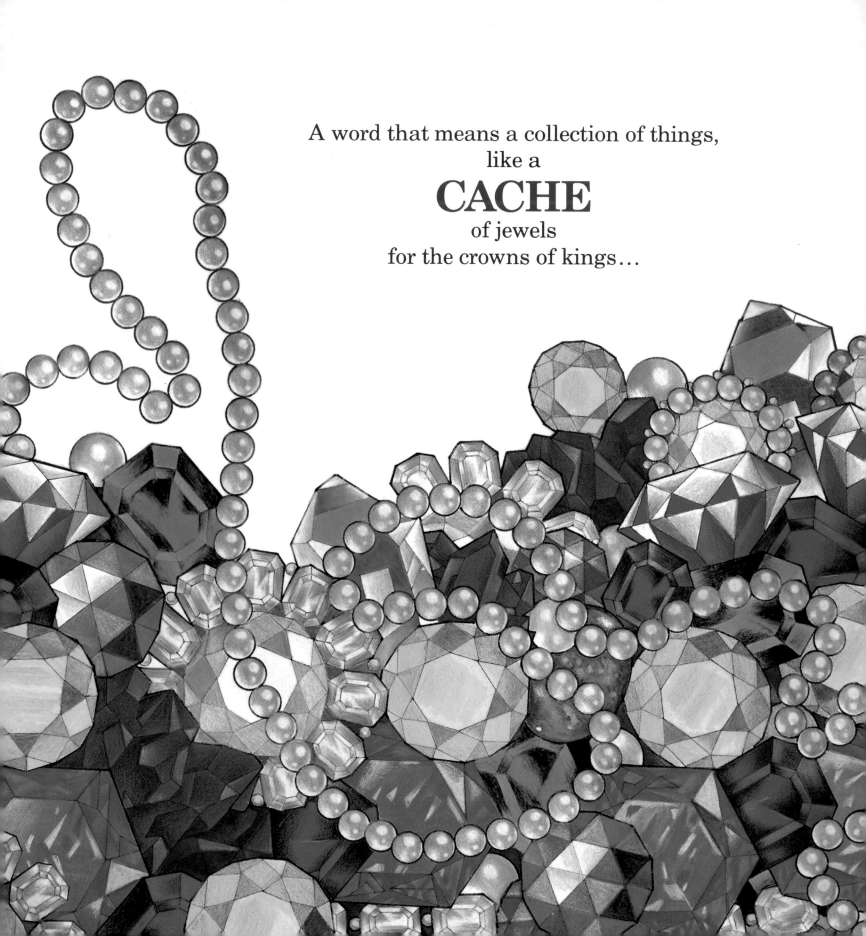

A word that means a collection of things,
like a

CACHE

of jewels
for the crowns of kings...

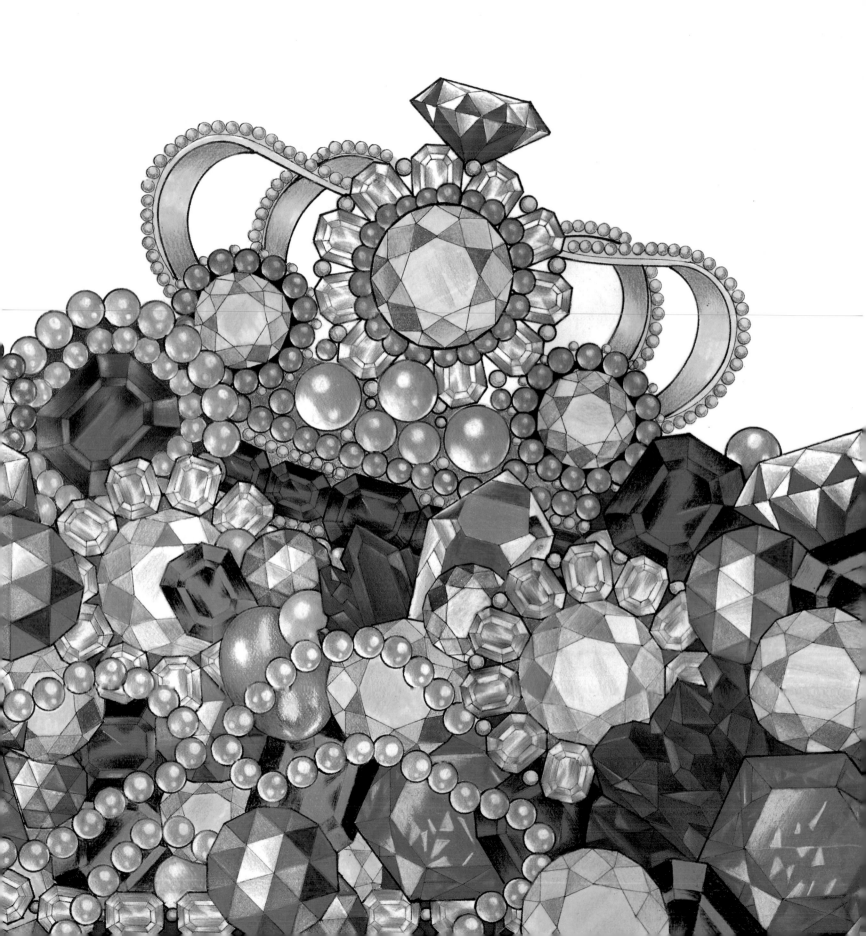

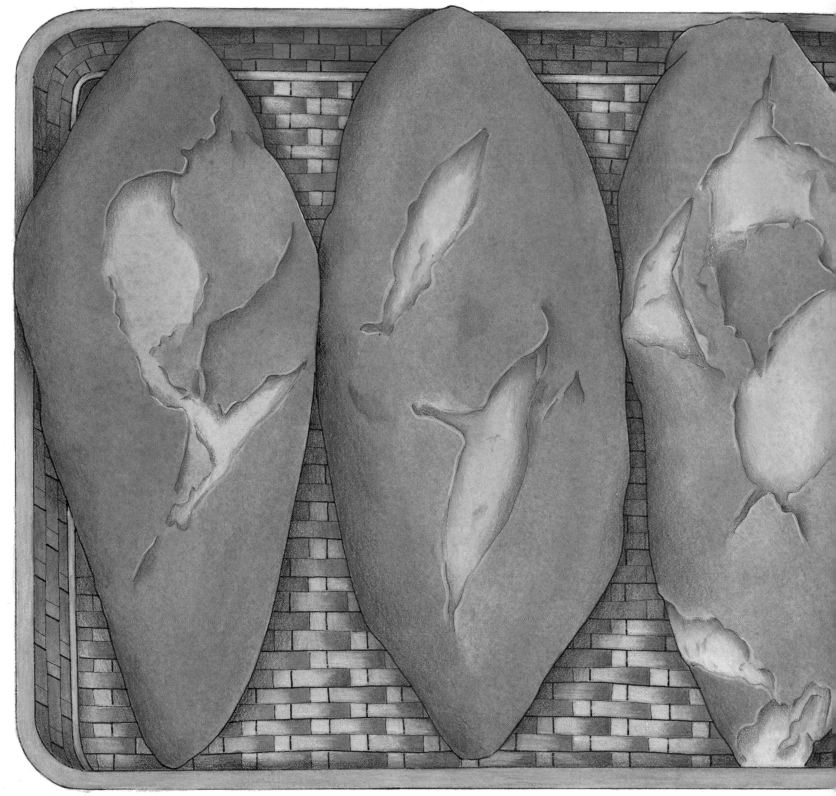

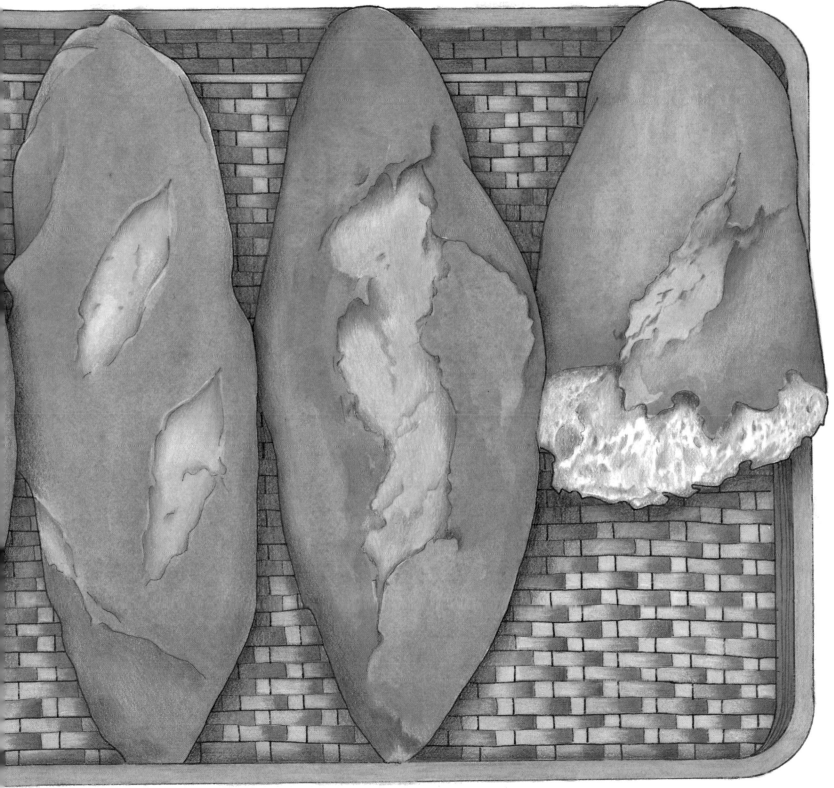

a **SCHOOL** of fish

a **GAM** of whales

a **FLEET** of ships
with
purple sails

a
CLUSTER
of
grapes

a
BEVY
of
beauties

.

all different

shapes

a **MUSTER** of peacocks

a
FLOCK
of
sheep

a
HOST
of
angels
fast
asleep

a **BOUQUET**
of flowers

a
SWARM
of
bees

a **KINDLE** of kittens
a **POD** of peas

a **PARCEL** of
penguins

a
FOREST
of
trees

a
COVEN
of
witches
as
scary
as
these

a **DRIFT** of swans

a **CLUMP**
of reeds

a
BED
of
oysters

a
STRING
of
beads

a **BROOD**
of
chicks

a **CLUTCH**
of
eggs

a
LITTER
of puppies on wobbly legs

a
PRIDE
of lions

a **LOCK** of hair

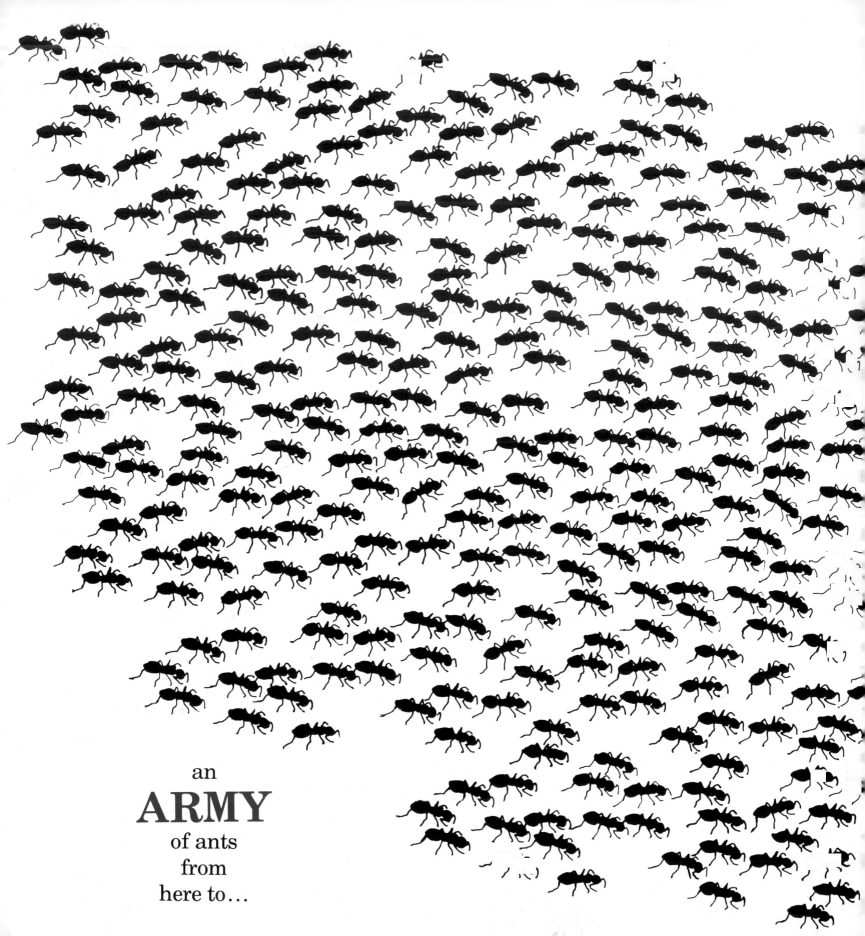

an
ARMY
of ants
from
here to…

there....

About five hundred years ago
knights and ladies in the know
used only very special words
to describe their flocks or herds.

These words are used by us today,
but some were lost along the way,
and new ones have been added too.

I've included quite a few.

And there are more of these group terms
like sleuth of bears
or clew of worms
or rafter of turkeys
walk of snails
leap of leopards
covey of quails.

But nouns aren't all collective,
and if I'm to be effective,
I'll tell about the other nouns
and adjectives and verbs.

All of them are parts of speech.

What fun!
I'll write a book for each.

—*Ruth Heller*

Note: One collective noun can describe many groups, as in a **host** of angels, daffodils, monks, thoughts, or sparrows.

One group can be described by more than one collective noun as in a **gam** of whales, a **mob** of whales, a **pod** of whales, a **school** of whales, or a **run** of whales.